# OLIVER
## TELLS A TALE

### BY K.P. BARNES

ISBN 978-1-955156-51-6 (paperback)
ISBN 978-1-955156-52-3 (hardcover)
ISBN 978-1-955156-53-0 (digital)

Rushmore Press LLC
1 800 460 9188
www.rushmorepress.com

Printed in the United States of America

Special thanks to:
Alexandria Hardy

Also thanks to:
Cheri May Barnes
Mike O'Rourke
Dan Hammersmith
Patti Quinn

"Oliver Christopher
David Magee,
come here... right now... on the double!"
I could tell by the way
mom used my full name
I was probably in big trouble!

OLiVeR CHRiSTOPHeR DAViD MAGee!

So I ran down the stairs
and saw mom standing there,
pointing toward the kitchen...
Not a word was said,
But her face was red,
And I noticed her left eye kept twitchin'.

What could it be?
What did she see
to make her look that way?
I had to find out
what this was about
before it wrecked my day.

I peeked through the door,

then down to the floor,

spilled milk, all over the place!

I turned to see

mom glaring at me

with a blameful look on her face.

"Oh this wasn't me,
you gotta believe,
I didn't make this mess!
I know I'm a kid,
but if I did,
surely I would confess!"

"Well if not you
then tell me who,"
mom asked, "who did all this?"
I had to think,
then in a blink,
A thought that couldn't miss!

"Maybe a cow
got in somehow,
I know they're full of the stuff!"
And that's when she
said angrily,
"Oliver, that is enough!"

17

"There was no cow,
no way, no how,
so stop all this foolishness!
now take my mop
and do not stop
until you clean up this mess!"
I nodded my head
and did as mom said,
I cleaned it up good-as-new...
Then ran back upstairs,
remembering there
was something I needed to do.

When I got to my room
I heard a "KABOOM!"
and then came a high pitched "YELP!"
I turned around
And ran back down,
knowing that mom would need help.

I heard it again
and ran to the den,
this time there was no surprise.
A broken vase...
things out of place...
mom wearing her ANGRY eyes!

And there by dad's chair,
not showing a care,
the little stray pup I let in.
His tongue hanging out,
Tail wagging about,
Grinning a puppy dog grin.
I wanted to say
that there was no way
I was to blame for this mess!
But I knew that she
would see right through me,
so I pleaded my case... more or less.

"I know this looks bad,
I know you and dad
said that I'm not ready yet...
but look at those eyes,
he's just the right size...
wouldn't he make a GREAT pet?"
I waited to see
if mom would agree,
"Oh what could she be thinking?"
she just stood there
with her MOM stare,
she wasn't even blinking!

A knock on the door
came just before
I thought she would finally speak up.
I ran to see
who it could be,
and mom quickly picked up the pup.

At the door looking in,
a half-hearted grin
and pigtails made things clear.
It was PESKY PEARL,
the neighbor girl,
but what was she doing here?

I opened the door
and couldn't ignore
the leash she had in her hand...
And knowing Pearl
like I know Pearl,
I figured she had something planned.

"I lost my dog,
my brand new dog,"
she said with a tear in her eye.
"We went out to play
and he ran away",
then she covered her face to cry.

"So sorry Pearl,
can't help ya girl,
but I wish ya luck... take care!"
I started to close
the door but then froze
when mom said "HOLD IT RIGHT THERE!"

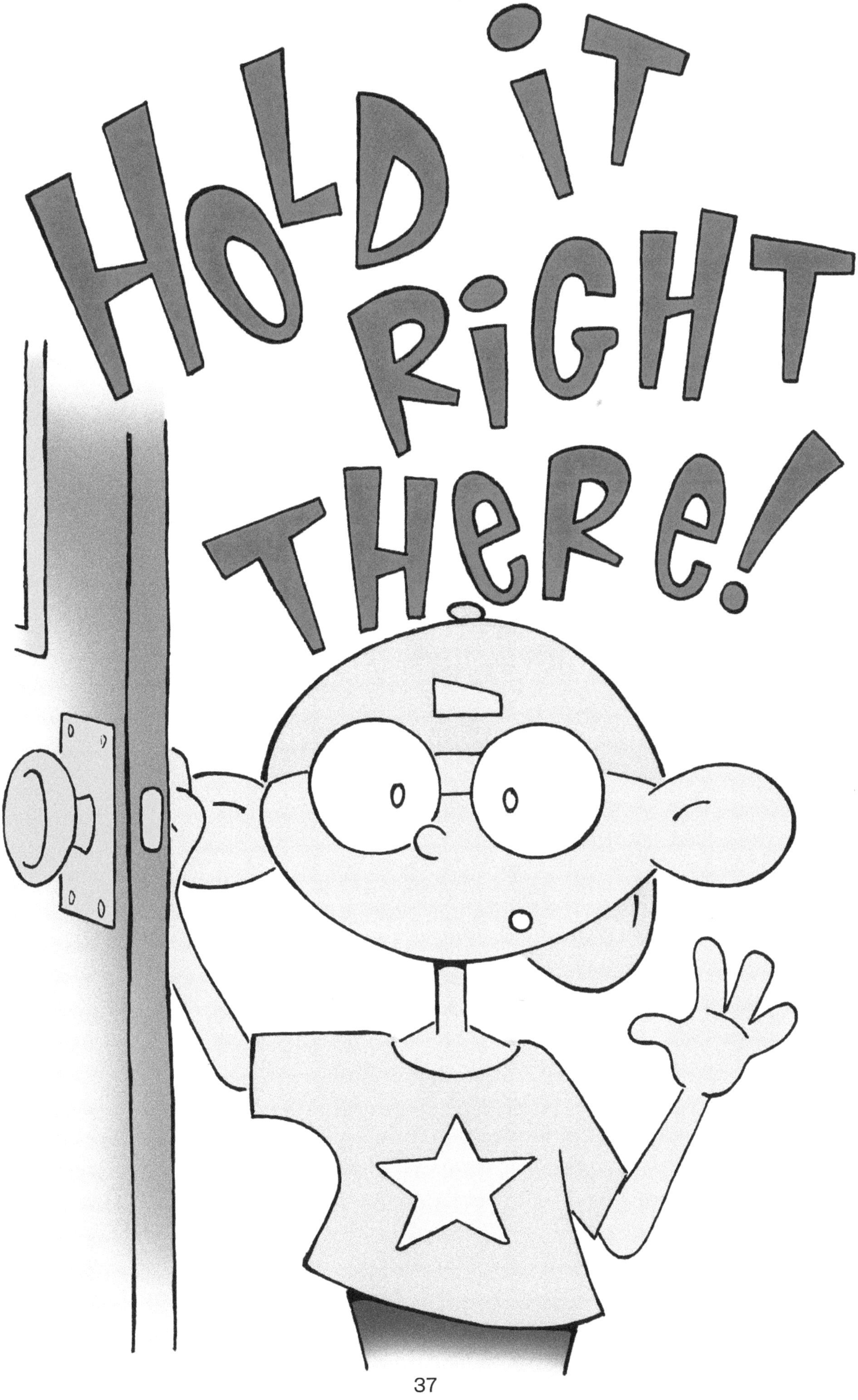
HOLD IT RIGHT THERE!

"Is this him, hon?
Is he the one
that you have been looking for?"
"It's him, it's him,
Oh yes, that's him...
that is my Sparky for sure!"

Mom gave her the pup
and helped leash him up,
but what Pearl did next really stung.
She said "thanks, Ms. Magee,"
and then turning to me
she rudely stuck out her tongue!

Mom closed the door,
boy was she sore!
I thought, "There's no way out of this!"
I'll be locked away
'til April or May...
or possibly until Christmas!

"Oliver, why?
Why did you lie
and tease poor Pearl that way?
I don't understand,
was this something planned?
WELL, what do YOU have to say?"
"I'm sorry I lied
and let him inside,
believe me, it's not what you think.
He was out on our lawn
and his collar was gone,
I just brought him in for a drink!"

# OLIVER WHY... WHY WHY DID YOU LIE?

"That still doesn't change
or begin to explain
your rudeness and dishonesty.
A pet must be earned
and you need to learn
RESPONSIBILITY!"
I could be good,
I knew I could,
I thought, "Piece of cake... no sweat!"
My mom will see
that I will be
the best kid that she's ever met!

At Dinner that night,

I ate every bite,

I even finished my peas!

And when mom brought dessert

I made sure to insert

A great big THANK YOU and PLEASE!

As the weeks went by,
I proved that I
was ready for my own pup.
I did as mom said,
Even made my own bed,
And always picked my toys up!
Then one Saturday,
mom took me away
to visit the local pet store...
And she let me get
My very own pet...

# A Fish Named Theodor!

CPSIA information can be obtained
at www.ICGtesting.com
Printed in the USA
BVHW021621010621
608547BV00007B/1412